The Counting Race

For my parents, Frank and Mary—MM

First Aladdin Paperbacks edition July 2003

Text copyright © 2003 by Simon & Schuster
Illustrations copyright © 2003 by Mike Gordon

ALADDIN PAPERBACKS
An imprint of Simon & Schuster Children's Publishing Division
1230 Avenue of the Americas, New York, New York 10020

Book design by Sammy Yuen Jr.
The text of this book was set in CentSchbook BT.

Printed in the United States of America
2 4 6 8 10 9 7 5 3 1

The Library of Congress Cataloging-in-Publication Data:
McNamara, Margaret.
The counting race / by Margaret McNamara ;
illustrated by Mike Gordon.—1st Aladdin Paperbacks ed.
p. cm. — (Robin Hill School)
Summary: When Mrs. Connor challenges her first–grade students to count to ten in less
than one second, they work together and find a way to count that will beat the clock.
ISBN 0-689-85539-7 (pbk.) — ISBN 0-689-85540-0 (library edition)
[1. Counting—Fiction. 2. Contests—Fiction. 3. Schools—Fiction.]
I. Gordon, Mike, ill. II. Title.
PZ7.M232518 Co 2003
[E]—dc21
2002008835

The Counting Race

Robin Hill School

Written by Margaret McNamara

Illustrated by Mike Gordon

Ready-to-Read

Aladdin Paperbacks

New York   London   Toronto   Sydney   Singapore

"We are having
a race today,"
said Mrs. Connor.

The first graders
loved races.

"A running race?"
asked Reza.

"An eating race?"
asked Katie.

"No," said Mrs. Connor,
"a counting race."
"What is a counting race?"
asked Hannah.

"I am going to see
if you can count to ten
in one second,"
said Mrs. Connor.

"That is so easy,"
said James.

"I'll go first,"
said Michael.
"One, two, three, four,
five, six—"

"Out of time,"
said Mrs. Connor.

"My turn," said Neil.
"One, two, three, four,
five, six, seven—"

"Sorry, Neil,"
said Mrs. Connor.

"Me next!" said Eigen.
"One, two, three, four,
five, six, seven, eight—"
"Close!" said Mrs. Connor.

Hannah put up her hand.
"Mrs. Connor, can all
the first graders
work on this
together?" she asked.

"Yes, Hannah,"
said Mrs. Connor.

All the first graders
got together.

They talked loudly.

They talked quietly.

They had an idea.

"Ask us to race again,
Mrs. Connor,"
said Megan.

"Okay," said Mrs. Connor.
"Can you count to ten
in one second?"

All together,
the first graders said,

"Two! Four!
Six! Eight!
Ten!"

"You did it,"
said Mrs. Connor.
"Good for you!"

"We counted by twos,"
said Emma.
"It is a faster way
to count," said James.

"Here is one more question,"
said Mrs. Connor.

"Two, four, six, eight.
Who do I appreciate?"
The children knew
the answer.

"Us!" they said.
And they were right again.